DATE DUE

Send Wendell

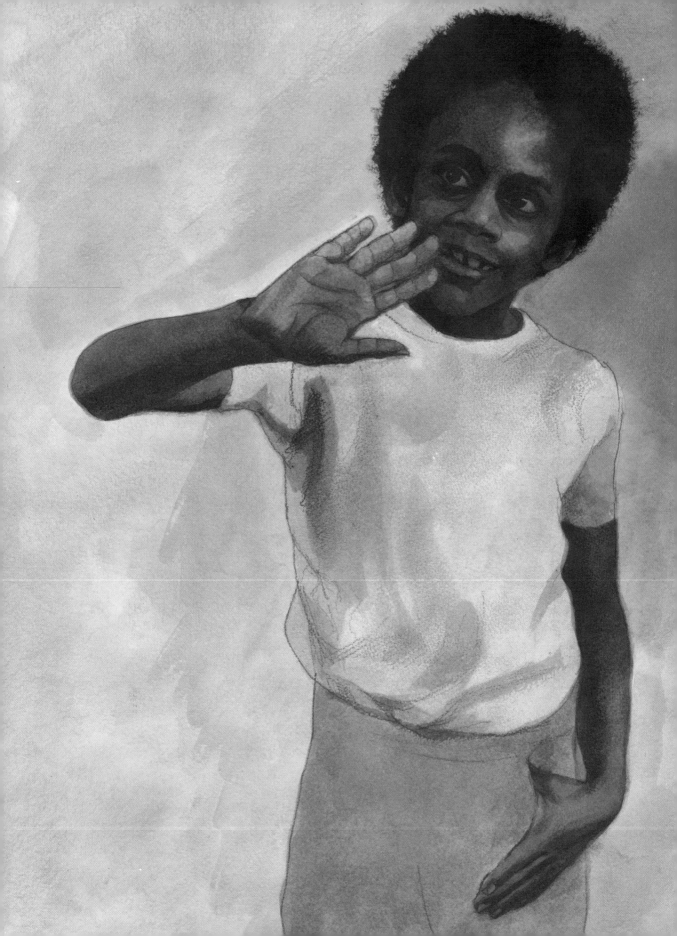

Send Wendell

by Genevieve Gray
drawings by Symeon Shimin

McGRAW-HILL BOOK COMPANY

New York • St. Louis • San Francisco • Düsseldorf
Johannesburg • Kuala Lumpur • London • Mexico
Montreal • New Delhi • Panama • Rio de Janeiro
Singapore • Sydney • Toronto

Library of Congress Cataloging in Publication Data

Gray, Genevieve
  Send Wendell.

    SUMMARY: Since the rest of the family is always
too busy, six-year-old Wendell does the errands all
the time until his uncle comes to visit.
    [1. Family life—Fiction] I. Shimin, Symeon,
illus. II. Title.
PZ7.G7774Sd   [E]   73-17414
ISBN 0-07-024195-3
ISBN 0-07-024196-1 (lib. bdg.)

456789 RABP 798765

*For Russ and Judy
and for Toby*

Wendell was a little boy six years old. He lived

in the first apartment

. . . on the top floor

. . . of the east wing

. . . of the last one

. . . of the four buildings

in the Project.

Every time Wendell went out by himself Mama

said, "Don't get lost!"

"I won't," said Wendell.

And he never did.

Wendell lived with Mama, Papa, William, Alice, James, Julie, and Walter. And the baby, Anthony. Mama and Papa and the children all liked each other and everybody laughed most of the time.

But even when a family is happy, there is always work to do. And Mama couldn't do all the work by herself.

"William," Mama would say, "put the clothes out on the line for me."

But William would put on his coat.

"I have to go play ball," William would say. "Send Wendell." And William would get his cap from the nail behind the door and leave.

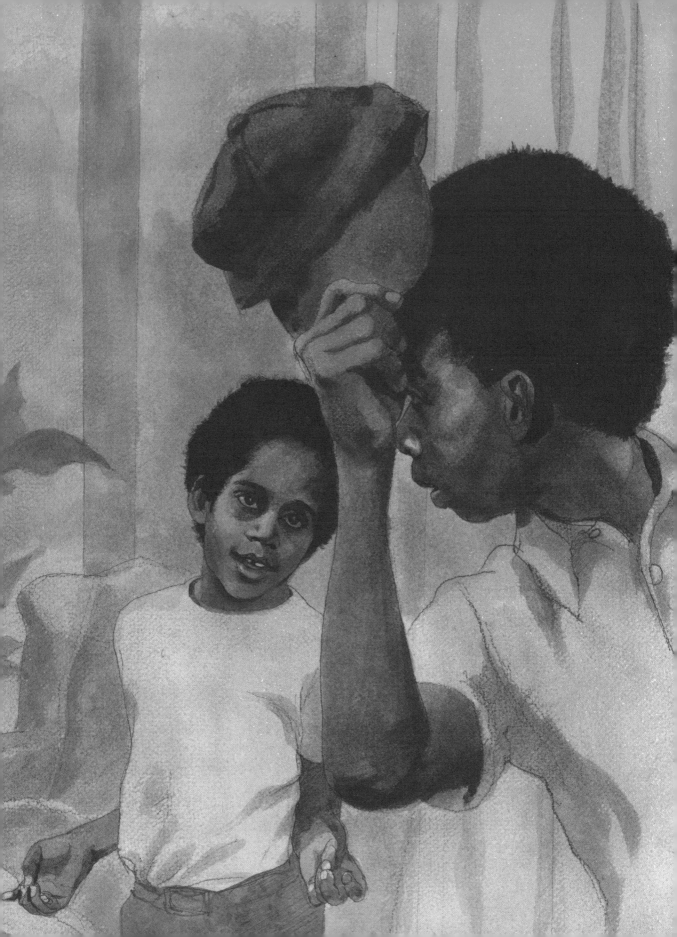

Or Mama would say, "Alice, go over to Mrs. Turner's. Ask her if she will let me have a cup of sugar."

"My boyfriend is coming to pick me up," Alice would say. "Send Wendell." And Alice would go to her room to see if her hair looked all right.

It was always the same. Mama might ask Papa to take out the garbage.

"I worked hard today," Papa would say. "Send Wendell."

Or Mama might ask Walter to go to the store for a loaf of bread.

"I'm too little," Walter would answer. "Send Wendell."

Wendell loved Mama very much and he liked to help her. But sometimes he wished—just a little bit— that Papa and William and Alice and James and Julie and Walter liked to help Mama as much as he did.

One day Mama said, "Julie, go down and see if
there is any mail."

"I have to put my doll to bed," said Julie. "Send
Wendell."

So Wendell started down to get the mail.

"Don't get lost!" said Mama.

"I won't," said Wendell.

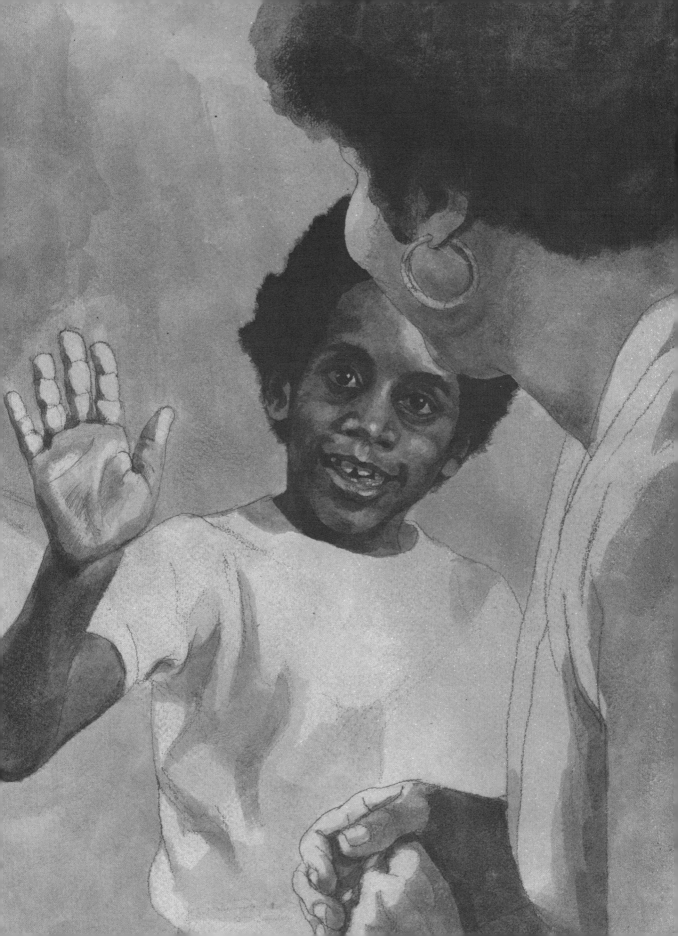

Down in the front hall of the building, Wendell looked in the box. There was a letter. He took it back and gave it to Mama.

Mama read the letter and laughed.

"Uncle Robert is coming to see us!" she said. "Think of that! All the way from California!" Then she laughed some more.

Wendell knew about Uncle Robert. He had a farm in California and made a lot of money. When James broke his leg, Uncle Robert sent the money to pay the bill. At Christmas time, the best presents under the tree were always from Uncle Robert.

But California was far away. No one in the family had ever seen Uncle Robert but Mama and Papa.

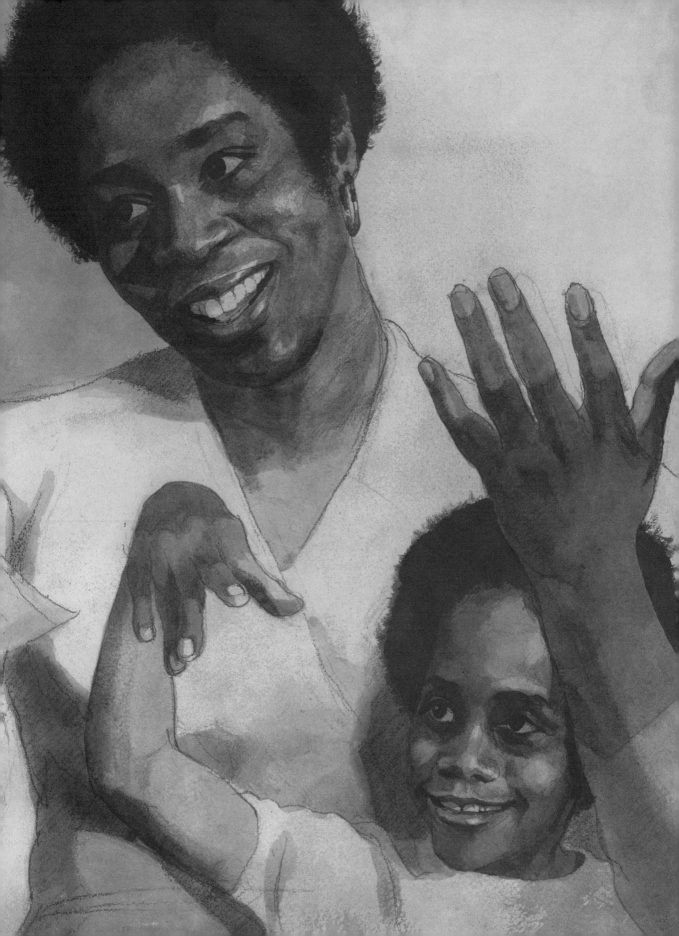

The days went by and the family got ready for
Uncle Robert. But Wendell did more to get ready
than anyone else, except Mama.

"Alice," said Mama. "Take the baby for a walk
while I get out the good dishes."

"I have to sew a button on my dress," said Alice.
"Send Wendell."

"James," said Mama. "Go over to Mrs. Sellers' place. Tell her I want to use her pretty cake pan."

"Teacher told me to work on my arithmetic," said James. "Send Wendell."

"William, go pick up Papa's good suit," said Mama. "It's down the street at the cleaner's."

"I just got home from school," said William. "Send Wendell."

Mama gave Wendell the money to pay the man at the cleaner's.

"Don't get lost!" said Mama.

"I won't," said Wendell.

Wendell went down to the first floor. There by the front door stood the biggest man Wendell had ever seen. The man was reading the names on all the boxes. He had on shiny black shoes and a shiny gold ring with a blue stone in it.

Wendell stopped still and stared up at the man. And the man turned and stared at Wendell.

Then the big man began to laugh, just like Mama.

"You must be James," he said.

"No, I'm Wendell," said Wendell.

"I'm your Uncle Robert," said the big man.

All of a sudden, Wendell began to feel nice inside. The nice feeling came out all over his face and he felt the corners of his mouth turn up.

"I'm going to the cleaner's for Mama," said Wendell. "I have to pick up Papa's good suit."

"You're a good boy to help out like that," said Uncle Robert. "I'll give you a ride."

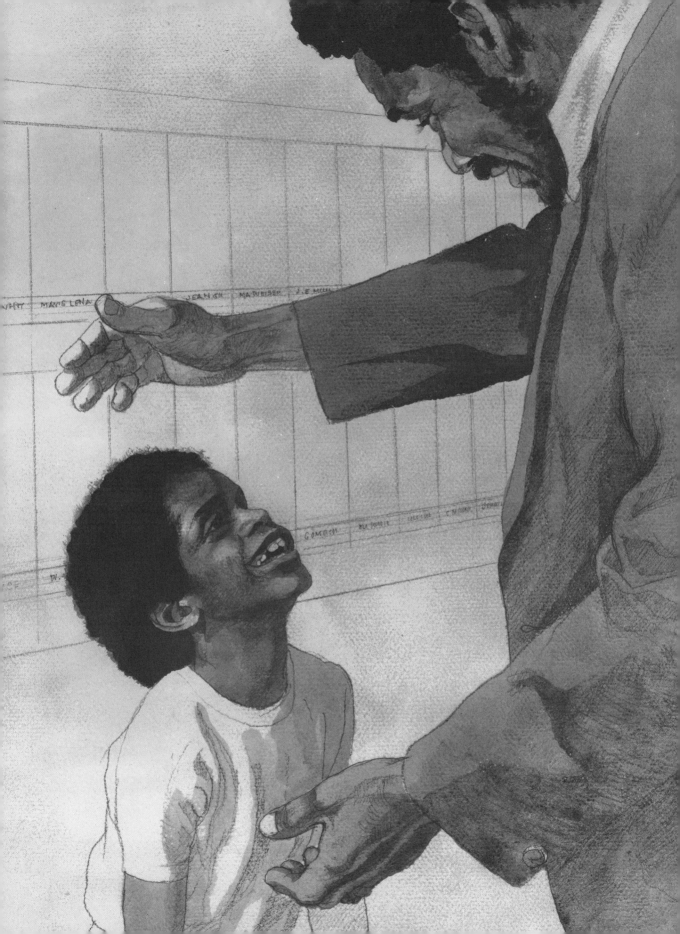

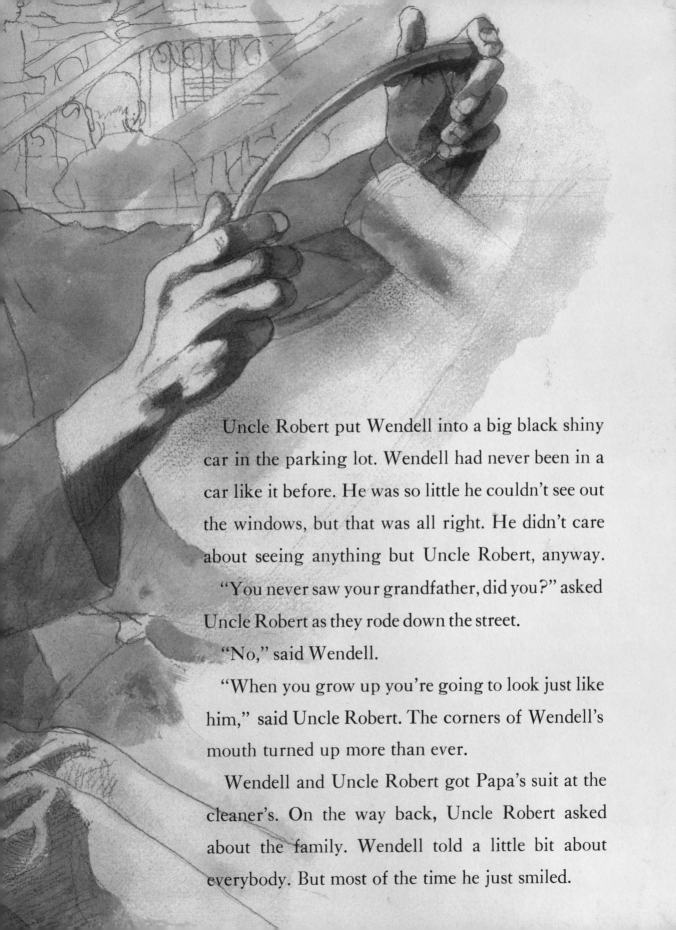

Uncle Robert put Wendell into a big black shiny car in the parking lot. Wendell had never been in a car like it before. He was so little he couldn't see out the windows, but that was all right. He didn't care about seeing anything but Uncle Robert, anyway.

"You never saw your grandfather, did you?" asked Uncle Robert as they rode down the street.

"No," said Wendell.

"When you grow up you're going to look just like him," said Uncle Robert. The corners of Wendell's mouth turned up more than ever.

Wendell and Uncle Robert got Papa's suit at the cleaner's. On the way back, Uncle Robert asked about the family. Wendell told a little bit about everybody. But most of the time he just smiled.

When Wendell and Uncle Robert got home, you never heard such laughing and talking. Mama was so glad to see Uncle Robert she put her arms around his neck and cried. Then Papa shook Uncle Robert's hand and patted him on the back. William and Alice and James and Julie and Walter all talked at once and jumped up and down.

The baby kicked off his covers and cried so somebody would look at him.

But no one did, not even Wendell.

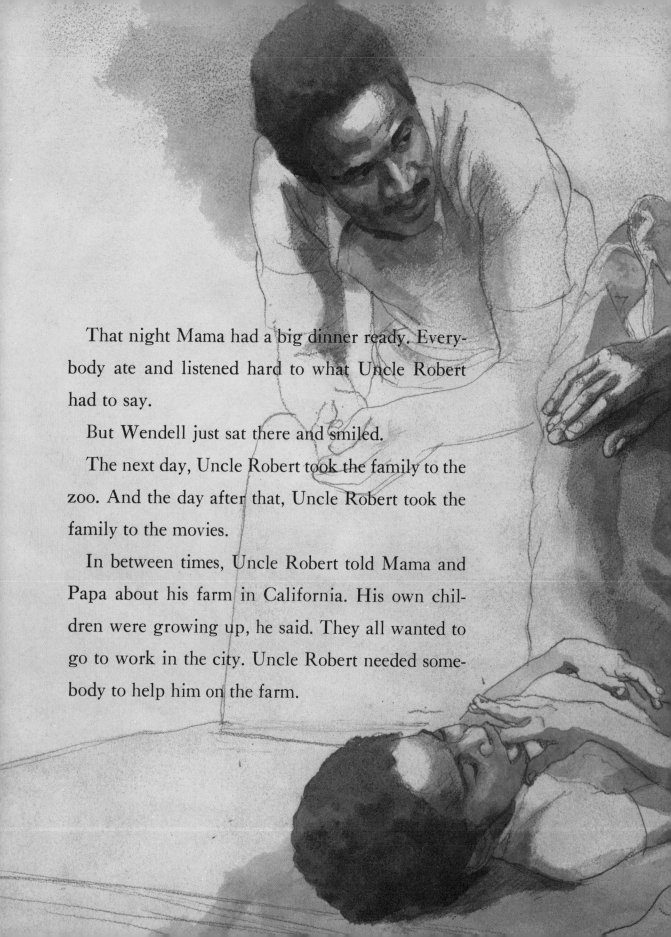

That night Mama had a big dinner ready. Everybody ate and listened hard to what Uncle Robert had to say.

But Wendell just sat there and smiled.

The next day, Uncle Robert took the family to the zoo. And the day after that, Uncle Robert took the family to the movies.

In between times, Uncle Robert told Mama and Papa about his farm in California. His own children were growing up, he said. They all wanted to go to work in the city. Uncle Robert needed somebody to help him on the farm.

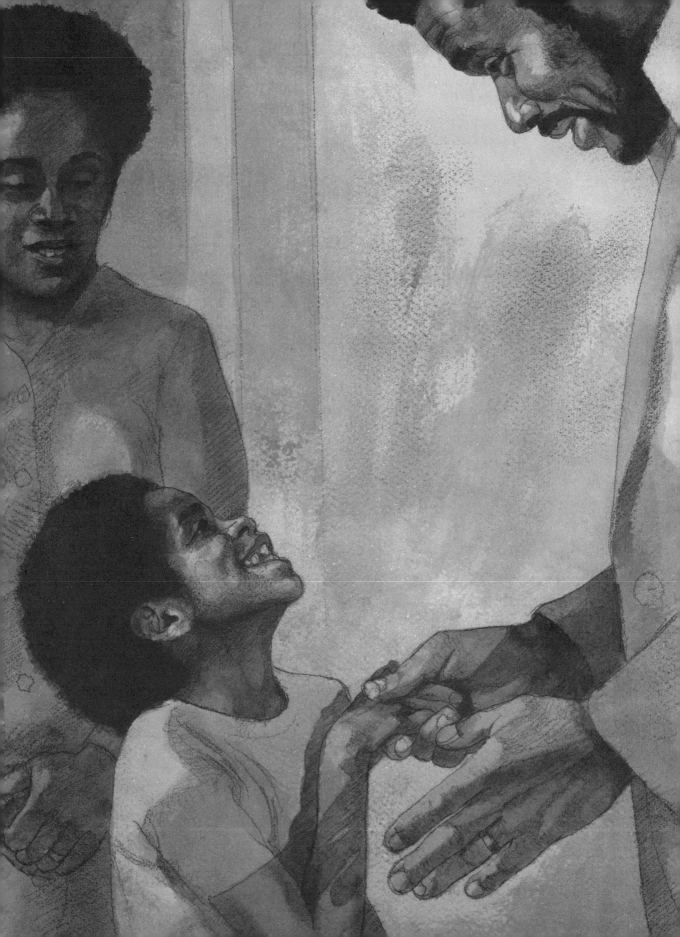

At last it was time for Uncle Robert to go back to California.

"Wendell," Uncle Robert said. "Your Mama and Papa say when you grow up a little more you can come help me on the farm. Do you want to come live in California?"

"Yes," said Wendell. And he held tight to Uncle Robert's hand.

The morning after Uncle Robert left, Mama was busy getting the apartment straight again.

"Alice," said Mama. "Mrs. Wilson gave me her ice trays to use while Uncle Robert was here. Take them back to her."

"I have to phone my girlfriend," said Alice. "Send Wendell."

But Wendell smiled. "I have to write a letter to Uncle Robert," he said.

And Mama made Alice go anyway.

"Don't get lost!" Mama said to Alice.

"Get *lost?*" said Alice, who was almost as big as Mama. "*Me?*"

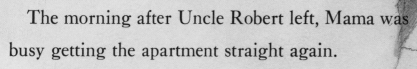

Wendell got a pencil and a piece of paper from the table drawer. At the top of the paper he wrote in big, careful letters,

DEAR UNCLE ROBERT

γ